To Cherry and Zora,
my very own Sproutling crew – T.J.

For Oscar – M.B.

First published 2016 by Macmillan Children's Books
This edition published 2017 by Macmillan Children's Books
an imprint of Pan Macmillan
20 New Wharf Road, London N1 9RR
Associated companies throughout the world
www.panmacmillan.com

ISBN: 978-1-5098-5400-4

3 5 7 9 8 6 4 2

A CIP catalogue record for this book is available from the British Library.

Printed in China

SPROUTZILLA
VS. CHRISTMAS

Written by
TOM JAMIESON

Illustrated by
MIKE BYRNE

MACMILLAN CHILDREN'S BOOKS

Jack loves Christmas.

He loves decorating the tree.

He loves singing carols.

He loves giving presents. (And receiving them is okay too!)

But there is one thing Jack doesn't like . . .

BRUSSELS SPROUTS.

Jack hated sprouts so much he'd never even eaten them.
And he never would. Unlike his sister Ruby.
"Eating sprouts will do you good," she said.

"I'd rather chew on a tyre whilst
tickling a tub full of tarantulas,"
said Jack. "Sprouts ruin Christmas!"

Jack couldn't imagine anything worse than eating them.
But there was something worse. Something much worse.

THE SPROUTS EATING YOU!

Which is what nearly
happened when his
parents brought home . . .

SPROUTZILLA.

He was the meanest, greenest Christmas ruining vegetable ever!

And things were about to get a lot worse as he stomped out the door with his army of Sproutlings.

In no time at all, they were . . .

SPLASHING,

SMASHING,

and CRASHING Christmas
EVERYWHERE!

With the sprouts on the rampage, everyone had been ordered to move inside – even the poor snowmen!

But there was one person with a very special
Christmas job who just couldn't stay inside.
And he was flying through the air straight towards . . .

SPROUTZILLA!

Oh no! He was mean and green –
and soon he would be gobbling up Santa!

Who could stop this mean, green menace?
Not the furious mums and dads,

not the extremely angry dinner ladies,

not even these boiling mad chefs.

SPROUTZILLA WAS UNSTOPPABLE.

As Sproutzilla got closer and closer to Santa, Jack and Ruby realised something. Frozen peas and even the stickiest puddings fired by extremely angry dinner ladies wouldn't stop him.

To save Christmas, Jack would have to do the one thing he had vowed never to do. Something worse than chewing on a tyre whilst tickling a tub of tarantulas . . .

He'd have to
EAT SPROUTS!

He didn't want to. But he did it.
Jack took a bite.
And then another.

He soon realised that sprouts
were sort of . . . kind of . . .

NOT BAD AT ALL!

At last, Sproutzilla was no more.
"See! I told you eating Brussels sprouts
would do you good," said Ruby.

"You did it. You stopped Sproutzilla!" cheered Santa. "Well done, you clever children. But ho, ho, no, Christmas isn't saved yet. I still have lots of presents to deliver and time is running out."

There had to be some way of getting Santa's sleigh back in the air. But how? Then Jack and Ruby's tummies started to rumble.

Luckily Santa knew what happens
when you eat lots and lots of sprouts.

"Quick. Hop on!" he cried, just as
Jack and Ruby let out a great big . . .

PAAAAAAAAAAAAAAAAAAAAARRRRRRRRRRRRP!

PAAAAAAAAAAAARRRRRRRRRRRRRP!

PAAAAAAARRRRRRRRRP!

Luckily there was just enough power to get every last present delivered.

In no time, the sleigh had landed
safely outside Jack and Ruby's house.
"We really did save Christmas!" smiled Jack.

Well maybe. You see, Sproutzilla had a friend . . .

TYRANNOPARSNIP-REX.